COFFEE WITH

MICHELANGELO

C O F F E E   W I T H

MICHELANGELO

JAMES HALL

FOREWORD BY JOHN JULIUS NORWICH

DUNCAN BAIRD PUBLISHERS

LONDON

Coffee with Michelangelo
James Hall

In memory of my father, Philip Hall

Distributed in the USA and Canada by
Sterling Publishing Co., Inc.
387 Park Avenue South
New York, NY 10016-8810

This edition first published in the UK and USA in 2007 by
Duncan Baird Publishers Ltd
Sixth Floor, Castle House
75–76 Wells Street, London W1T 3QH

Managing Editors: Peggy Vance and Gill Paul
Co-ordinating Editors: Daphne Razazan and James Hodgson
Editor: Jack Tresidder
Assistant Editor: Kirty Topiwala
Managing Designer: Clare Thorpe

Library of Congress Cataloging-in-Publication Data Available
ISBN-10: 1-84483-511-1   ISBN-13: 978-1-84483-511-9
10 9 8 7 6 5 4 3 2 1
Printed in China

For information about custom editions, special sales, premium and corporate
purchases, please contact Sterling Special Sales Department at 800-805-5489
or specialsales@sterlingpub.com.

Publisher's note:
The interviews in this book are purely fictional, while having a solid basis in
biographical fact. They take place between a fictionalized Michelangelo and
an imaginary interviewer.

CONTENTS

Foreword by JOHN JULIUS NORWICH

The first thing to be said about geniuses is that they are never nice people. Michelangelo alone could be said to have summed up the whole Renaissance: sculptor, painter, architect, poet—there seemed to be nothing he couldn't do. As a man, however, he was a nightmare. He did his colleagues down whenever he could. He commissioned his own authorized biography, carefully omitting his apprenticeship to Ghirlandaio. And he was a thundering snob. In 1546 we find him ordering his nephew to "persuade Gismondo to return to Florence, so that it should no longer be said that I have a brother at Settignano who plods after oxen."

When Charles VIII of France invaded Italy in 1494, Michelangelo promptly fled the city—the first of his several flights from real or imagined dangers—

leaving his patron Piero de' Medici in the lurch.
Then there was trouble in Rome, where a statue
sold as antique turned out to be his own, artificially
distressed. Five years later in Florence, he ruthlessly
beat off the competition of Andrea Sansovino to work
on a huge and superb block of Carrara marble for
the republican government. Back in Rome again, he
blamed the endless difficulties over the tomb of Pope
Julius II on the intrigues of his rival Bramante and
of the young Raphael, whom he detested. In fact the
difficulties were, to a considerable degree, of
his own making, and there is little doubt that he
retained considerable sums of money for work he
never delivered.

And so the list goes on: but the second thing
to be said about geniuses is that they must be
forgiven. That initial visit to Rome produced, when
Michelangelo was still only 25, the great *Pietà* in

St. Peter's. Had he not got rid of Sansovino, we should never have had the *David*. Had Pope Julius II listened to his violent protestations that he was a sculptor rather than a painter—which he considered a vastly inferior form of life—the Sistine Chapel would have been different indeed from what it is today. And these are only the ultimate miracles: Michelangelo was to create a dozen or more others, each of which, if produced by any of his leading contemporaries, would be considered his masterpiece. True, the tomb of Pope Julius—with its intended 40 full-size statues—proved over-ambitious even for him, particularly after (as he might have foreseen) the pope's death in 1513 cut off most of the funds; but nothing that gave rise to that astonishing *Moses* can be seen as a complete failure.

As an architect, Michelangelo most memorably gave us the Capitoline Square in Rome and the dome of St. Peter's. Neither of them did he live to complete, though both probably look more or less as he envisaged them. Much of his poetry, too, survives only in fragments—did any great artist leave so much unfinished work behind him?

But who cares? He was Michelangelo. He rests his case.

John Julius Norwich.

INTRODUCTION

The idea of "interviewing" Michelangelo nearly
four and a half centuries after his death may sound
strange, but to Italians of the 16th century a semi-
fictional dialogue was the standard format in which
to introduce a subject to a wider audience. Despite a
reputation for being a truculent loner, Michelangelo
was clearly a lively conversationalist when in
congenial company. He was an eloquent "speaker"
in two dialogues compiled in the 1540s, one by the
Portuguese artist Francisco da Holanda, the other
by the Florentine political exile Donato Giannotti.

The dialogue in this book is a hybrid composed
from a variety of sources—the contemporary
biographies by Giorgio Vasari and Ascanio Condivi;
Michelangelo's many letters and poems; anecdotes
and quotations relayed by contemporaries. The rest

consists of all those things which I think he could plausibly have said. I have based my dialogue on a number of notional conversations with him in Rome between his move there to paint the *Last Judgment* and his death 30 years later, at what was then the phenomenal age of 88. Here he looks back on an amazingly long career as an artist—always with total conviction, if not total accuracy.

It is hard to imagine a better subject for an interview. A poet as well as an unsurpassed sculptor, painter, and architect, Michelangelo lived during an extraordinary period in Italian history. He was highly opinionated and articulate, did not suffer fools and rivals gladly, and had a notoriously dry wit. Psychologically, he exists in a state of perpetual internal exile; he is passionate to a fault, loving and hating his own land and its culture in equal measure; and he is not averse to consigning his contemporaries to Hell (literally so in the case of the papal functionary whose features adorn Minos in the *Last Judgment*).

The fiercest critics of Michelangelo have tended to portray him as a warped tunnel-visionary, greedy for fame, money, boys, and social advancement. I hope this book will show that in addition to being the greatest of all artists, Michelangelo was a man of courage and integrity.

MICHELANGELO (1475–1564)
His Life in Short

Michelangelo Buonarroti was born in the small
village of Caprese, near Arezzo, on March 6, 1475.
In his seventies, he told his pupil and biographer,
Ascanio Condivi, that at his birth the position of
the planets Mercury, Venus, and Jupiter foretold
that he would be a genius "in those arts that delight
the senses." As the horoscope has since been shown
to be a year out, this story may have been a figment
of Michelangelo's own vivid imagination. Even so,
it attests powerfully to his own sense of purpose.
He did not take up art by accident or to make money:
he felt he had been specifically chosen by God to use
his talent to accomplish great things.

    Michelangelo was the second son of Lodovico di
Leonardo Buonarroti Simoni and his wife, Francesca

di Neri Miniato del Sera. His father, a Florentine who was serving a short term as mayor of Caprese, moved back to the family home near the church of Santa Croce, Florence, soon after the birth, and the new baby was sent to a wet-nurse at the family farm in Settignano, a few miles outside Florence. His mother, Francesca, died in 1481, having given birth to three more sons, but is never once mentioned by Michelangelo.

Until the 15th century, the Buonarroti had been relatively prosperous through small-scale money-lending, but their fortunes had since declined and their meagre income now derived chiefly from the small farm at Settignano. Michelangelo's father was too proud and prickly to embark on a serious career (the brief posting as mayor was one of his few jobs), and was dismayed when his second son neglected his school-work in order to draw, as the visual arts were traditionally regarded as manual trades. But Michelangelo prevailed (perhaps because he was already making money from selling drawings), and in 1487 his presence was recorded in the studio of the leading Florentine painters Domenico and Davide Ghirlandaio. His father arranged a three-year apprenticeship for him the following year.

About a year later, Michelangelo was talent-spotted by the Medici, the de facto rulers of Florence, and joined Lorenzo de' Medici's household, furthering his artistic studies in their sculpture garden near San Marco, under the tutelage of the sculptor Bertoldo. Surviving from this period are two marble reliefs, the *Madonna of the Stairs* and the *Battle of the Centaurs* (both Florence, Casa Buonarroti). The subject of the latter was suggested by Angelo Poliziano, the most celebrated classical scholar and poet in Italy. Michelangelo's own love of writing and reading poetry was fostered in this highly cultivated milieu.

Lorenzo de' Medici died in 1492, but Michelangelo continued to work for his less politically astute son Piero. He carved a statue of *Hercules* (now lost) and began his lifelong study of human anatomy by witnessing a dissection. When the French invaded Italy in 1494 and threatened Florence, Michelangelo was so terrified by a friend's dream in which a bedraggled Lorenzo de' Medici warned of impending disaster that he fled the city, traveling first to Venice and then Bologna. Encouraged by the fiery Dominican preacher Girolamo Savonarola, the Florentines expelled Piero, and established the first Florentine Republic, with Savonarola as its spiritual leader. Michelangelo returned briefly to the city, carving a statue of the city's patron saint *St. John the Baptist* (lost) before moving on to Rome in 1496.

He was summoned there by the immensely wealthy papal chancellor, Cardinal Raffaele Riario, who had been duped by a dealer into buying a fake antiquity of a *Sleeping Cupid* (lost) carved and artificially aged by Michelangelo. On discovering the deception, Riario sought out the artist, and immediately commissioned Michelangelo to carve a marble *Bacchus* (Florence, Bargello) for his own sculpture garden, which was filled with antiquities. The cardinal was dismayed by the tipsy appearance of the wine god and sold the sculpture on to his (and Michelangelo's) banker Jacopo Galli, who put it in his own sculpture garden. Galli continued to support the artist, and in 1497 helped secure the commission for a marble *Pietà* to adorn the tomb of a French cardinal in a chapel adjoining St. Peter's.

In the autumn of 1497, Michelangelo left Rome for the quarries of Carrara, northwest of Florence, to select a suitable piece of marble, and he remained there until the following spring. This was the first of many visits to the quarries in search of the best-quality stone. Completed in 1500, the *Pietà* (Rome, St. Peter's) is a meticulously finished tour de force and Michelangelo's first great public success; it is his only work to be signed (on the Virgin's sash). He was now much in demand, and wealthy enough to subsidize his impecunious family in Florence (which itself created tensions, especially with his irascible father), and to make investments.

In 1501, he returned to Florence to carve the marble *David* (Florence, Accademia), the first colossal nude since antiquity. More than 13 feet high, it was installed to great acclaim outside the Palazzo della Signoria, seat of the republican government, in 1504. Its frankly delineated genitals and elegantly coiffeured pubic hair were, however, immediately covered up by a gilt garland. Michelangelo was beginning to attract foreign patrons, and made a bronze *David* (lost) for a favorite of the French king, and a statue of the *Madonna and Child* (Bruges, Notre Dame) for Flemish cloth merchants. Spectacular new commissions poured in, but from now on his career is littered with incomplete projects: the demands made by patrons, and Michelangelo's tendency to think big, then bigger, could be counter-productive.

It is now that lines of poetry—his own, as well as that of Petrarch and other Tuscan greats—start to be inscribed on his drawings. In one of the earliest, a rhyming couplet written alongside a study of the right arm of *David*, he compares the challenge of carving the sculpture with that of David in fighting Goliath. This heroic vision of the sculptor's task is a riposte to those (such as Leonardo da Vinci) who dismissed it as dirty manual labor. In these same years Michelangelo made three "tondi"—circular images of the Madonna and Child. The *Pitti Tondo* (Florence, Bargello) and the *Taddei Tondo* (London, Royal Academy of Arts) were carved in marble and were left unfinished; the *Doni Tondo* (Florence, Uffizi) is Michelangelo's only complete painting on panel to survive.

In 1503, he was asked to carve twelve over-life-size marble Apostles for the cathedral, and then in 1504 came another commission from the Florentine Republic for a fresco of a battle scene, probably 19 × 58 feet, for a wall in the new council hall in the Palazzo della Signoria. His highly influential cartoon in black chalk for the central section of the *Battle of Cascina* (now destroyed) showed Florentine soldiers called to arms while they were bathing in the Arno. The fresco was meant to complement another battle scene by Leonardo da Vinci, but was never executed because the newly elected Pope Julius II summoned Michelangelo to Rome in 1505 to begin work on a gigantic tomb for himself. From now on, the popes would be his principal patrons, and they made him the highest paid artist in the world.

Michelangelo designed a monument to outstrip the ancients, three stories high, with around 40 statues and many reliefs. From May to December 1505 he was in Carrara securing marble, and while there he toyed with the idea of carving a colossal sculpture into the side of a mountain. However, his return to Rome was to be brief. The expense of Pope Julius' planned wars of conquest

in central Italy, his simultaneous decision to rebuild
St. Peter's, and his desire that Michelangelo paint
the Sistine Ceiling, meant that work on the tomb
was likely to be suspended, and in April 1506 the
disillusioned sculptor secretly left for Florence.
Defying papal letters ordering him to return to
Rome, he started carving *St. Matthew* (Florence,
Accademia), one of the Apostles, for the cathedral.
But to prevent a diplomatic row developing,
Michelangelo was sent to Bologna to apologize
to Julius who had just captured the city. He was
forgiven, and charged with the formidable task of
modeling and casting a colossal seated bronze statue
of the pope to be placed above the main door of
Bologna cathedral. Completed in 1508, it survived
only three years. In 1511 papal forces were expelled
from Bologna, and the statue was melted down to
make a large cannon called "La Giulia," a nickname

contemptuously referring to the pope.

In 1508, Michelangelo was summoned to Rome to paint frescoes on the vault of the Sistine Chapel, and spent the next four years creating the world's first great ceiling painting. Pope Julius died in 1513, to be succeeded by the Medici Pope Leo X, who initially favored Raphael—not just because he preferred the younger artist's more charming style, but also because he found Michelangelo difficult to deal with. A revised contract was drawn up with Pope Julius' heirs for his tomb in 1513, and Michelangelo began carving three sculptures for it: *Moses* (Rome, San Pietro in Vincoli), the *Dying Slave*, and the *Awakening Slave* (both Paris, Louvre). A third contract was signed in 1516. Each time the overall size of the tomb was reduced, as the political power of the former pope's family, and Michelangelo's available time, dwindled. In 1514, he also signed a contract to carve a statue of the *Risen Christ* for the church of Santa Maria Sopra Minerva in Rome, which would be completed in 1521 (in situ).

Work on Julius' tomb was again interrupted in 1516, when Pope Leo persuaded Michelangelo to return to Florence, once more under Medici rule, to make a spectacular façade for the Medici church of San Lorenzo. This was Michelangelo's first major architectural commission, though it also featured numerous statues and reliefs. The commission was canceled in 1519, owing to spiraling costs and changed priorities, allowing Michelangelo to continue work on the tomb, this time carving a new and larger series of *Slaves* (Florence, Accademia). In 1518, he ordered an associate in Rome to burn any "chartoni" in his studio—probably the cartoons made for the Sistine Ceiling. Many more drawings would be destroyed during the course of his life.

Such was Michelangelo's fame that in 1520 Count Alessandro da Canossa wrote to him claiming him as an esteemed relative, and Michelangelo was only too happy to endorse the idea that he had noble lineage.

Before the new series of *Slaves* could be finished, Michelangelo was told to design a new sacristy for San Lorenzo, to house tombs for four members of the Medici family. Work on the so-called Medici Chapel was repeatedly interrupted. The death of Pope Leo in 1521 brought work to a halt, but it was resumed in 1523 when another Medici was elected pope—Clement VII. In 1524 he was also commissioned to build a library in San Lorenzo to house Lorenzo de' Medici's celebrated collection of manuscripts and books. Work in San Lorenzo was again interrupted when Rome was sacked by an Imperial army in 1527, and Pope Clement forced to flee. The Medici were expelled from Florence and a second Florentine

Republic established. Michelangelo took charge of the city's fortifications and made designs for defensive bastions. In 1529, his uncertainty about the political situation caused him to flee briefly to Venice. When Medici rule was re-established in the summer of 1530, Michelangelo went into hiding but was pardoned by Pope Clement VII, and resumed work at San Lorenzo. He also carved a statue of *Apollo* (Florence, Bargello) for the new governor of Florence, Baccio Valori.

Michelangelo's father—with whom he had a very stormy relationship—died in 1531, and Michelangelo wrote two poems in his memory. In the same year he had completed a panel painting, *Leda and the Swan* (lost), for Duke Alfonso d'Este but refused to hand it over on account of the superciliousness of the duke's representative. The following year, a fourth contract was signed for the Julius tomb, and during a long visit to Rome he met and fell in love with a handsome teenage nobleman, Tommaso de' Cavalieri, to whom he wrote many love poems, and made some spectacular drawings on mythological subjects (mostly Windsor, Royal Collection). In the early 1530s, Michelangelo's Rome-based Florentine banker friend Luigi del Riccio circulated fair copies of Michelangelo's poems with the ultimate intention of publishing a collection, but the project foundered after Riccio's death in 1546. In 1532, the poet Ariosto called Michelangelo "il divino" in his epic poem *Orlando Furioso*, the first of many such accolades.

Michelangelo left Florence for good in 1534, with the work at San Lorenzo still unfinished. He was out of sympathy with the new Medici regime in Florence, and may already have been asked to paint the *Last Judgment* on the altar wall of the Sistine Chapel. Pope Clement died in September, but the new Farnese

Pope Paul III appointed Michelangelo supreme architect, sculptor, and painter to the papal palace, and confirmed the commission for the *Last Judgment*. Work began in earnest in 1536, once the pope issued a decree releasing him temporarily from his obligation to work on the Julius tomb. At around this time he met the devout aristocrat and poet Vittoria Colonna, for whom he made several drawings of the life of Christ (London, British Museum; Boston, Isabella Stewart Gardner Museum) and wrote many poems. The *Last Judgment* (45 × 40 feet) was completed in 1541, with around 400 figures. It was immediately acclaimed, and reproductive engravings spread its fame throughout Europe, but the many nude figures proved controversial. In 1550, the Venetian writer Pietro Aretino, having unsuccessfully solicited Michelangelo for some drawings, published a letter in which he denounced the indecency of the fresco, and accused him of embezzling money meant for Pope Julius' tomb. The controversy would lead, shortly after Michelangelo's death, to the fresco being repainted with clothing and loin-cloths.

In around 1540 Michelangelo, who was friendly with a group of exiled Florentine republicans living in Rome, started work on a bust of the classical republican hero *Brutus* (Florence, Bargello) to celebrate the murder in 1537 of the autocratic ruler of Florence, Duke Alessandro de' Medici. In 1542, the fifth and final contract was signed for the Julius tomb, and in 1545 a much reduced version was erected, not in St. Peter's but in the church of San Pietro in Vincoli, Rome. The statue of *Moses* (initially planned as a corner figure on the first story) was now the center-piece; the local Jewish population queued up to see it and pay their respects. In the same year, the Medici Chapel was cobbled together in Florence using the unfinished statues that Michelangelo left behind, and others completed by assistants.

Many appeals had been made to Michelangelo to return to Florence, or at the very least to give instructions on how the Medici Chapel should be completed, but he declined to cooperate, in part because he disapproved of Grand Duke Cosimo I de' Medici. The Medici Chapel became a haven for artists, and writers conducted imaginary conversations with the allegorical statues. Michelangelo replied to one poem in which *Night* is made to speak with a lugubrious poem of his own.

In 1544 and 1546 he fell seriously ill, and was cared for in the Roman palace of the Florentine exile Roberto Strozzi, who was rewarded with the two *Slaves* (Paris, Louvre) made for the superseded second version of the Julius tomb.

In 1537, Michelangelo had been consulted on how to rationalize the Campidoglio, the square on top of the Capitoline Hill, and in 1546 he was appointed architect to St. Peter's. From now on architecture—less physically demanding than sculpture or painting—occupied most of his time. In the same year, the Farnese Pope Paul III ordered him to complete the Palazzo Farnese in Rome. The Medici library at San Lorenzo could not be completed until after 1558 when he finally sent a model of the staircase to Florence.

Michelangelo revolutionized everything he touched, but his radicalism was nowhere more apparent than in his architecture. Even Vasari was shocked by his flouting of classical norms at San Lorenzo: he said those influenced by it had produced architecture "more grotesque than rational or disciplined."

Michelangelo's last paintings were two frescoes: the *Conversion of Saul* and the *Crucifixion of St. Peter* (each 19 × 20 feet) for the Pauline Chapel in the Vatican. Completed in 1550 when he was 74, they were his least ingratiating works, with ponderous figures and austere colors.

Michelangelo's Florentine contemporaries had no doubt about his greatness. In 1546, the Florentine historian and poet Benedetto Varchi lectured on Michelangelo's poetry in Santa Maria Novella, Florence, publishing his lecture in 1549. In 1550, Giorgio Vasari published the first edition of the *Lives of the Artists*, and Michelangelo was the only living artist to be included. It was unheard of for an artist to have a biography published in their own lifetime. Despite Vasari's contention that Michelangelo represented the pinnacle of achievement in all the arts, superior even to the ancients, Michelangelo was infuriated by several aspects of his book. In 1553, he authorized his studio assistant, Ascanio Condivi, to publish a biography "correcting" Vasari on a number of points, while other issues were clarified. Michelangelo was now said to have been a virtual autodidact in his youth, learning nothing from his contemporaries. He was, Condivi said, never to blame for the "tragedy" of Pope Julius' tomb, and had been left out of pocket; it was the fault of patrons if any commissions did not materialize; he was neither mean nor secretive and unsociable; he had no impure thoughts about boys.

From around 1550 until his death in 1564, Michelangelo was increasingly concerned with his own spiritual salvation. In 1550, we hear the first mention of the Florentine *Pietà* (Florence, Museo dell'Opera del Duomo), a large marble group which was probably meant for his own tomb, but which he partially mutilated after finding a flaw in the marble. In around 1552, he began the so-called *Rondanini Pietà* (Milan, Castello Sforzesco), which was to be his last sculpture, but this also remained unfinished. In addition, he made several tremulous drawings of the Crucifixion, probably for private devotion (London, British Museum; Paris, Louvre etc.). In 1550 he made a special pilgrimage to seven churches in Rome, and in 1556 he began a pilgrimage to the House of Mary at Loreto, but was summoned back to Rome by the pope before he could get there. His significant charitable gifts date from the late 1540s, and he also claimed publicly that he worked on St. Peter's "for the love of God" rather than for a salary. He was, however, receiving a huge monthly stipend from the pope, which was at least twelve times more than what Titian was being paid for paintings by the king of Spain.

Michelangelo died in Rome on February 18, 1564, aged 88. He was attended by, among others, Tommaso de' Cavalieri, now married and with two children. The body was taken back to Florence. Vasari and the members of the Florentine Accademia del Disegno (founded in 1563, with Michelangelo unanimously voted an honorary member) arranged for the coffin to be taken to Michelangelo's parish church of Santa Croce in a torch-lit procession, and there the lid was opened. Miraculously—considering that Michelangelo had been dead for 22 days—the corpse was said to be not in the least bit decomposed, and this was taken as a sign of his sanctity. The crowd filed past to touch the great man's face.

Grand Duke Cosimo I Medici had been dismayed to learn that Michelangelo had burned the drawings in his Rome studio before he died—"an act unworthy of him"—for now there was no trace of his plans for the incomplete Medici projects in Florence. But the ruler of Florence still allowed a grandiose memorial service to be held on July 14 in the Medici family church of San Lorenzo, organized by the Accademia, which provided temporary floats and paintings of key episodes from his life. Benedetto Varchi gave a long funeral oration which was immediately published. The Accademia then set to work on an elaborate tomb, which was unveiled in Santa Croce in 1575. It was paid for by his nephew and sole heir, Leonardo Buonarroti.

NOW LET'S START TALKING ...

Over the following pages, Michelangelo engages in an imaginary conversation covering twelve themes, responding freely to searching questions.

The questions are in green italic type;
Michelangelo's answers are in brown type.

THE SELF-TAUGHT REBEL

Michelangelo was the first artist to insist he was an untutored genius, rebelling against authority and against his age. This trait has proved especially popular since the Romantic period, though traditionalists usually preferred the more malleable and less original Raphael as a model for the aspiring artist. Michelangelo's determination to deny that any artists had taught him eventually forced Vasari to publish a document proving he had trained in the Ghirlandaio workshop. We still don't know how he learned to carve, but in Florence it was not so unusual for artists to quickly master a new skill.

Maestro, thank you for agreeing to set the record straight. Could I first ask how and why you became an artist?

Like most sons of good families, I was sent to a grammar school where they taught reading and writing, in Latin as well as in the vernacular. I wasn't a very diligent pupil, and was much more interested in drawing. I was also keen on sculpture, and used to watch the stonemasons at work in the famous quarries near our farm in Settignano. As a baby, I'd been sent to a wet nurse there who was the daughter and wife of stonemasons. That's why I always say I sucked in with my nurse's milk my sculptor's chisels and hammer.

My father, who disdained work that involved manual exertion, was appalled when he found that I wanted to become an artist, especially as I would have excelled at any other career I'd chosen. He beat me regularly, but less often when I started to make money from selling drawings, some of which (unbeknown to him) were copies of works by famous masters, with the paper artificially aged. We certainly needed the money, and there wasn't much likelihood that my other brothers would make any. The real turning point came when, at the age of 12, my father apprenticed me to the painters Domenico and Davide Ghirlandaio, and then a year or so later I was talent-spotted by Lorenzo de' Medici. I went to live in his household, and studied in the Medici sculpture garden near San Marco.

What did you learn in the Ghirlandaio workshop?

Very little. You know what their stuff's like. The Ghirlandaio brothers and their large team of assistants produced frescoes and altarpieces by

the yard. Very competent, of course—they won't
fall apart or fade, like Leonardo's. But they're so
banal. Stately line-ups of pretty people, nicely kitted
out with designer clothes and accessories, and
surrounded by fashionable furniture and fittings.
Worst of all are the flattering portraits of patrons
and celebrities inserted into biblical narratives
at every opportunity, and the genteel landscape
backgrounds. The indiscriminate love of cute detail
derives from Flemish art, and this is just the kind of
work that appeals to women (especially the very old
and very young), friars and nuns, and nobles with
no feeling for harmony. Of course, the Ghirlandaio
brothers didn't really like or understand me. They
were jealous. They took one look at my drawings and
realized they were too powerful to conform to their
brand. They were furious when I took a drawing
of some draped female figures done by another

apprentice and redid the contours with a thicker pen, making them weightier and more vibrant.

But surely some good did come of it, for didn't they encourage you to draw regularly, and to study antiquities and frescoes by earlier Florentine artists, such as Giotto and Masaccio?

Yes, of course, they did encourage us, and I learned sound fresco and panel painting technique from them as well. But don't be misled. The Ghirlandaio brothers only ever paid lip-service to the great Florentines and to the ancients. They never venerated them as I do, emulating that severe simplicity whereby figures and actions are stripped down to an essential core. Their interest was merely part of a magpie approach that afflicts so much recent art. Jacks-of-all-trades, their quotations from Masaccio or from antiquity are picturesque details thrown into a fundamentally Flemish stew. I've no objection to depicting things like plants or animals or clothes—I'm very proud of my blades of grass in the *Doni Tondo*, of the owl that accompanies *Night* in the Medici Chapel, and Lorenzo de' Medici's elaborate armor—but these are all just accessories. What judge is there who cannot understand that a man's foot is more noble than his shoe, and his skin more noble than the sheep's skin from which his clothes are made?

Unfortunately, today's artists are obsessed by debased examples of nature, and put them center stage. Leonardo, Raphael, and Titian spent far too much time looking at perfumed courtiers, in and out of fancy clothes. And poor old Albrecht Dürer only ever looked at Germans! No wonder their art is so vulgar, unfocused, and diffuse. We live in a decadent age, and the Ghirlandaio brothers can take much of the blame.

You moved on to the Medici sculpture garden. Was this any better?

Lorenzo invited promising artists to join his household, and we were encouraged to broaden our horizons and think for ourselves. The garden was surrounded by arcaded loggias filled with antiquities, and we also had access to the Medici collections of modern art. Lorenzo was keen to encourage sculptors, because since the death of Andrea del Verrocchio in 1488 there was a dearth of good sculptors in Florence. Everyone in the household dined together, so you didn't just talk to artists, who are rarely educated or articulate. I met great scholars and poets like Angelo Poliziano, who'd been a tutor to Lorenzo's children. I talked about Dante and Petrarch with him, and he came up with subjects for me, usually taken from classical mythology. He suggested the subject of my relief, the *Battle of the Centaurs*—though, of course, I didn't follow the story slavishly. I also copied and restored antique sculpture. Bertoldo, the sculptor who oversaw the garden, worked in bronze, so people often ask how I learned to carve in stone. I taught myself the basic rudiments from watching others, in Settignano and Florence. Carving marble is breathtakingly simple. There's no complex chemistry involved. The most important thing is to understand the potential of each block of stone, and to plan thoroughly in advance with drawings and with wax and clay models. And you have to be very strong.

What training did you have in architecture?

Medieval architects usually rose from the ranks of masons, after serving an apprenticeship in a quarry, but ever since, the education of leading architects has been much more broadly based. Visual artists make the best architects because they're experts in the arts of design, and need to make architectural backdrops and frameworks for their works. Brunelleschi was a goldsmith and sculptor by training, Bramante a painter. My first major experience of architecture came with designing the vast architectural component of Pope Julius' tomb, and I also designed the painted architectural framework for the Sistine Ceiling. This was vital for the ceiling's success, and gives it its taut, rolling rhythm. I know what goes on in quarries, so in that respect I'm far more traditionally educated than most, and I have a very good relationship with the masons and carpenters who work on my building sites. The best architects produce drawings and clay models, but leave it to others to turn them into detailed plans and a building. I always say the compasses should be in the eyes, not the hand.

THE BODY BEAUTIFUL

The male nude is central to Michelangelo's art, and he was uniquely preoccupied by it. Ever since, whoever tackles the male nude has to tackle Michelangelo, and only Caravaggio and Rodin have found really convincing variations on the "Michelangelo-esque." The subject can seem rather specialized, and a Venetian contemporary complained that if you've seen one of Michelangelo's figures, you've seen them all. But throughout his life he wrought countless variations on his beloved theme, almost never repeating a pose, gesture, or emotional nuance.

Maestro, can you explain your fascination with the male nude—a preoccupation which lasts uninterrupted from the beginning to the end of your career?

The one true subject of art is the heroic male figure, his actions and passions. The two basic prototypes for the heroic male nude are, on the one hand, Adam, and on the other, Christ. Everything you need is there.

Your male nudes, especially the early ones, are of unsurpassed beauty. One thinks of the dead Christ in the St. Peter's Pietà, the marble David, and the ignudi and Adam of the Sistine Ceiling. How are viewers supposed to respond to this beauty?

The male body is God's greatest creation, and when His own son was incarnated He became a man—not a woman, not a horse, and not a tree. Christ was the most beautiful man who ever lived, and this is why every time we see male beauty we approach the divine. We're not just entitled, we're duty-bound to worship it.

Even before Christ was incarnated, God paved the way for his arrival by inspiring the ancient Greeks and Romans to venerate the male body. They were pagans, and so couldn't be fully conscious of it, but their greatest statues of the male nude all predict the coming of Christ. Thus, the *Apollo* foretells Christ the redeemer, and the *Laocoön* foretells Christ in his passion. Pope Julius brought these sculptures to the Vatican and always regarded them as sermons in stone.

My own art frequently draws on Christianity's visual pre-history. My sculpture of St. Matthew and my drawing of Christ on the Cross are inspired by

the *Laocoön*, which I saw when it was being excavated;
while the upper part of Adam on the Sistine Ceiling is
inspired by the *Apollo*.

*That's fascinating—but no other artist has been so
exclusively focused on the male nude. And some of
your contemporaries have been troubled by all this
nudity. The genitals of your statue of David were quickly
covered up, and there's talk, I understand, of censoring
the* Last Judgment.

The male nude is intrinsically good and Christian,
and should not be covered up because a few
misguided souls—whether male or female—become
physically inflamed. It's certainly true that we
worshipers of the male body have sometimes
let ourselves down. The ancient Greeks engaged
in physical relationships with boys, and we

Florentines have a reputation for this kind of thing throughout Europe.

But the basic principle that older men should act as mentors to the young is entirely honorable, and these male friendships should not be discredited because of a few lapses. The philosopher and priest Marsilio Ficino was a member of Lorenzo de' Medici's household, and he invented the term "Platonic love" for same-sex relationships—the boy enjoys the beauty of the man's intellect, and the man enjoys the beauty of the boy's youthful body. Ficino deplored physical relationships, and I've always endeavored to extinguish in the young any unseemly and unbridled desire which might spring up. The artist must be as saintly as possible if the Holy Spirit is to inspire him. In my work I rarely depict young boys. My male nudes tend to be somewhere between boyhood and their early 30s—the ideal age at which

Christ died, and at which we will be resurrected on the last day.

So if people find, say, the Last Judgment *impious or obscene, that's their fault?*

When the papal Master of Ceremonies, Biagio da Cesena, complained to the pope that I was filling the papal chapel with scandalous figures, I gave his features to Minos, Judge of the Underworld, the figure whose genitals are being bitten by a snake. Only now does Biagio understand that the resurrection of the dead involves our being reclothed in flesh. There's no mention of our being clothed in sheep's skin from head to toe! We must stand naked before God. If my male figures are so often nude, this is because it's always, in some sense, Judgment Day.

But your vision of an all-male society which worships the male nude still leaves little place for women. Where do they fit in?

We all know that Eve was a mixed blessing. The ancients actually believed that Arcadia was exclusively male, and that Arcadian men lived long and carefree lives, eating a diet of acorns. It was only later that women appeared on the scene, starting with Pandora and her box of tricks. The male *ignudi* on the Sistine Ceiling, holding their sheaves of acorns, are meant in part to evoke this all-male golden age, and when Adam is created he seems to belong with them, as he's of similar scale and physique. All men, I think, yearn from time to time to return to this all-male golden age, and are troubled by the idea of women. That's not to say there aren't great exceptions to prove the rule. The Virgin Mary

canceled out the sin of Eve, and my illustrious friend
Vittoria Colonna is as chaste as she is beautiful. I
wrote a madrigal for her which begins: "A man in
a woman, in fact a god speaks through her mouth."
There are plenty of women among the blessed in the
Last Judgment, and the damned are all men.

THE LINE OF GENIUS

For Florentine artists of the Renaissance,
drawing was the father of all art forms.
Because of its close connection with writing,
mathematics, and scientific or technical
illustration, proficiency in drawing bolstered
the claim that painting and sculpture were
intellectual rather than manual arts. When
people today ask of a contemporary artist,
"but can s/he draw?", they are keepers of
this Florentine flame. For Michelangelo's
contemporaries, his supremacy stemmed from
his skill as a draftsman. Even when very old
he would sit shoeless, drawing for three-hour
stretches, and he urged his pupils to follow
his example.

*Maestro, gazing at all these incredible drawings, piled
up everywhere, here in your studio in Rome, I feel as if
I'm at the nerve-center of your art.*

Of course you do. We Florentines call drawing
disegno, which means "design." Through
drawing we think, we plan, we solve. A Florentine
is born, as it were, with a silver pen in his mouth.
Florence has the highest literacy rates in the
world, and in Dante and Petrarch, Boccaccio
and Poliziano, the greatest writers since antiquity.
We prize drawing with the same fervor that
we prize writing, and that's why we also have
the best painters and sculptors since antiquity.
Without drawing, you can't do anything of
lasting value.

   The first public displays of drawings took
place in Florence. Leonardo showed a full-scale

cartoon of the *Madonna and Child with St. Anne*, and we both displayed cartoons for battle frescoes in the council chamber. Everyone hailed them as a school for all the world, though most came to see my *Battle of Cascina*, and were so keen to have a memento that they eventually tore the drawing to pieces. You can contrast us Florentines with those devious and frivolous Venetians. They don't have any decent writers—the best that they can offer is that scurrilous buffoon, Aretino. And their artists don't even draw. They paint directly onto the canvas. That's why Titian is always so wishy-washy, his figures completely boneless.

So you're saying then that in your work the two great Florentine traditions of drawing and writing actively come together.

Literally so, as in many cases I often jot down lines of poetry next to my drawings.

Let me see ... Ah, there it is (*taking a drawing from the nearest pile*). That's a study for the right arm of the marble *David*. The rhyming couplet next to the arm, written in elegant italic script, is one of my earliest poems. It's like a personal inscription—"David with the sling and I with the bow. Michelangelo." I was in my early 20s, and this was the commission of a lifetime. I was comparing the task of carving the gigantic block of marble, aided by a bow-drill, with David's struggle against the giant Goliath. And just below it I've quoted a line from Petrarch. For me, writing and drawing are parallel enterprises. They are of equal distinction and beauty. But until I came along, writers had far more prestige than artists. Incidentally, I know Dante's works off by heart, even the *Paradiso*.

Choose any Canto at random, and I'll recite it from beginning to end.

I'd love to put you to the test. But I'd like to ask you another question first. I've noticed that you place a lot of importance on drawing from life. Why don't you just draw from memory?

You have to start with nature. Nature is the source. All the great Florentines and the ancients became great by looking at nature—in its grandest aspects. The one true subject of art is the heroic male figure, and to portray it convincingly you need to have a nude body before you, breathing and moving, pressing against itself and its surroundings. Of course, you don't just transcribe exactly what you see, but unless you feel the pulse and heartbeat, your art's an empty shell. I ought to add that constant life drawing with sketch-books has only really been possible in my lifetime, for now we have plentiful supplies of relatively cheap paper made from rags. This is due to the invention of printing in the last century and the consequent vast expansion of the book trade. But I'm still frugal enough to fill a whole page with sketches, and I often write shopping lists on the back.

Your Battle of Cascina *cartoon was put on public display, but wasn't that because you had to leave in a hurry to go to Rome to make Pope Julius' tomb? Usually you're very secretive about your drawings, and have been known to burn them.*

That's right. I don't want other artists to see or steal my ideas when they're only in sketch form. I'm quite happy to show finished drawings, however. I make cartoons for painter friends to turn into pictures. I've also recently done a series of mythological narratives, and some images of Christ, which I gave away as gifts to close friends of mine like Tommaso de' Cavalieri and Vittoria Colonna. Cavalieri was learning to draw and I sent the drawings to him as part of an informal correspondence course that I devised for him.

But when you're planning a work, and especially sculpture or architecture, you make wax and clay models as well as drawings. There are plenty lying around here, too. You won the commission for the David *by showing a small wax model of what you proposed to do, and you also make full-scale clay models. Which comes first, the sketch or the sketch-model?*

There's no sense of priority, and sometimes the model comes first—after all, the Bible doesn't mention God needing to make a drawing before he modeled Adam out of earth. Painters often need wax or clay models, too, and I used to make models for Ghirlandaio so he could study a pose and the fall of drapery. Too many sculptors can't draw, and too many painters can't model. Any artist worthy of the name will be as adept at model-making as they are at drawing.

CUTTING EDGE

Michelangelo's unrivaled command of male
anatomy was underpinned by anatomical
dissections. He planned to make an illustrated
anatomical treatise with the celebrated surgeon
Realdo Colombo, and a separate illustrated
treatise for artists focusing on the movements
and gestures of the human body. Neither was
ever published. For all those who praised his
anatomical skill, however, there were others
who complained that his nudes looked flayed,
because of the prominence of some of the
muscles and veins. In reality, Michelangelo's
intimate knowledge of the human body
gave him the confidence to make supremely
expressive distortions.

Maestro, when we spoke yesterday about your drawings
of live models, we didn't mention that you also make
drawings of dead models.

Yes, in fact I'm going to a dissection this afternoon.
My great anatomist friend, Realdo Colombo, who's
now doing an autopsy on Ignatius of Loyola, founder
of the Jesuits, has just offered me the body of a
handsome young Moorish pirate who died before
he could be sold as a slave. Dissection has to be
done quickly, because we have no preservatives, and
bodies decompose very fast, especially in summer.
Why don't you come along and watch?

It's a very kind offer, but I just don't have the stomach
for this sort of thing.

I quite understand, and I can tell you it doesn't get

any easier. I'm going to have to give up soon because my stomach can't handle it. The Moor may well be my last anatomy—unless Colombo comes up with something extra special, like a pope or a cardinal. In response to your question, I first became actively involved in dissection when I was part of Lorenzo de' Medici's household. The Prior of Santo Spirito in Florence allowed me to participate in a dissection after I carved a wooden crucifix for him. The corpse came from a hospital that was affiliated to the church, and we dissected it in a room provided by the Prior. A detailed understanding of the inside as well as the outside of the human body is vital for any artist, as you can see by looking at antique sculpture. The ancients had an unparalleled knowledge of anatomy, but that knowledge was lost during the Dark Ages.

So the Church approves of anatomical dissection?

Ever since some heretics, known as the Cathars,
claimed there were two Gods, a "good" God of spirit,
and an "evil" God of matter, the more enlightened
churchmen have supported the natural sciences,
insofar as science can show that God's creation is
good in every way. Dissection of corpses helps us all
to appreciate the miracle that is the human body.
The ancients were guided by the same principle.
The great anatomist Galen thought anatomy was the
source of a perfect theology, and that everyone should
know about it. For me, marveling at human anatomy
is a form of worship. Christ's incarnation is a vote
of confidence in human anatomy, and when people
marvel at the body of Christ in my St. Peter's *Pietà*,
I want them to marvel at the beauty of his anatomy.

Marveling at human anatomy from the outside, as
it were, is very different from marveling at it from the

inside. Performing dissections repeatedly, as you do, must be a form of penance—because dissecting a body is so unpleasant and gruelling.

Absolutely. Nothing makes me think more about death. And by sensing what's beneath the skin, the viewer of my work should think about the imminence of death, too.

So your lifelong interest in anatomical dissection is not simply utilitarian. After all, there's no obvious reason why an awareness of the appearance of the interior of a corpse should be relevant to the representation of living bodies in vigorous action.

You exaggerate. A living, moving body is always in some respects a blur. You have to know what to look for, what's actually under the skin if you're to offer a convincing representation of it. This is the only way to strip away the camouflage of conventional vision.

At the same time, your art isn't simply naturalistic. Your contours almost have a life of their own, and I can't help noticing that you pay most attention to the male torso, and that you exaggerate its size and importance. Does your idealization of the torso stem from your anatomical knowledge?

The torso is the crossroads that connects brain with genitals, arms with legs, top with bottom, and left with right. It contains by far the largest concentration of muscles and vital organs—above all, the heart. Dissection has brought this home to me. Realdo Colombo is celebrated for his public dissections of live animals, and I too have performed the occasional vivisection—only then do you really understand the importance of the heart. The emotional intensity of my works is due to the fact that their focal point is the heart, the engine of feeling. I agree with a saying attributed to Socrates that "the human breast should have been furnished with open windows, so that men might not keep their feelings concealed, but have them open to view." I try to open a window onto the human heart.

You showed me earlier a drawing for the male allegorical figure of Day, *in the Medici Chapel, in which you'd drawn a face on his stomach and chest. Why?*

That was a joke, of course, but it's nonetheless true that what other artists seek out in the human face, I find in the human torso. This is why I've rarely been interested in doing portraits, and why the heads of my figures twist sharply away to the side, so it's harder to see eye to eye with them. However lovely, the face tends to be too changeable to represent any enduring human essence. I believe that if you can't see the human heart and anchor yourself in it, then you won't find any truth worth having. The human face is like the crest of the wave—striking and even intensely beautiful, but frothy.

So despite your great experience of anatomy you don't have a holistic view of the human body. You seem reluctant to show us the human heart and face together—in a single view, as Leonardo did in his image of the Vitruvian Man.

Who can honestly believe in a becalmed image of the human condition? We've forsaken the human heart and we have to find it again. We must be lion-hearted if we're to save ourselves on Judgment Day.

DIVINE OR VERY HUMAN?

Michelangelo was the most revered and rewarded artist of his age, but his sharp tongue and proud, suspicious nature could make him difficult to deal with. His combination of talent and turbulence has made him the epitome of the tormented genius. At the same time, his burning desire to "restore" his family's fortunes and prestige made him even more prickly—and acquisitive. The fact that he was only too happy to accept the Count of Canossa's unfounded claim that they were related showed how susceptible he was to the lure of social advancement.

*Maestro, I've heard some of your contemporaries
calling you "divino angelo." What exactly do they
mean by this?*

It's just a terrible half pun. In his so-called
biography of me, Giorgio Vasari says I'm "divine"
because my birth horoscope showed that marvelous
works would issue from my hand. *Divino* is an
accolade usually only handed out to a saint, and
I'm certainly no saint, though I try my utmost to
serve God, who determined the position of the
planets at my birth. If I've made anything of value
it's by God's grace.

*Yet you're quite an individualist. You deny
learning anything much from your teachers or your
contemporaries, and you show little sympathy for
other artists.*

Is it my fault that we live in a dark age? I'm really just a traditionalist. I would gladly have sat at the knee of Lorenzo Ghiberti or of Donatello, who both died before I was born. Ghiberti turned Florence from an artistic backwater into a new Athens. His two sets of bronze doors for the Baptistery, to which he devoted his life, are wonders of art and of pious ambition. It was I who dubbed the second set the Gates of Paradise, because of their unsurpassed beauty. But Ghiberti's significance as an artist goes beyond the doors. He's the first to have written an autobiography, and there he sets out his vision of the artist as far more than a jobbing tradesman. The Ghibertian artist must study nature and antiquity, and must be a philosopher—above all, he must live for art, not money. Donatello was very different, but no less inspirational. He's the most versatile and influential of 15th-century artists—my earliest surviving relief, the *Madonna of the Stairs*, is a homage to him. He was always brusque and to the point, with a sharp tongue and ready wit. He didn't put up with nonsense from patrons, however great, or from other artists. He paid so little attention to money or to his appearance that Cosimo de' Medici gave him a red cloak with a hood, but after wearing it once or twice, he put it aside because it made him look too foppish.

So you embody aspects of both Ghiberti and Donatello—highly literary and intellectual, but blunt and unkempt.

When I'm working, which is nearly all of the time, I think only of the work at hand. I go without food and sleep, and when I do sleep, I sleep in my clothes. Look at my legs. I'm now wearing boots of dog skin next to my skin. I haven't taken them off for months, and when I do eventually remove them, some of my skin will come away. I don't want to be interrupted when I'm working, and I always say I serve the pope much better by being in my studio than by hanging around at his court. I'm married to my art, and my works are my children. It's outrageous when obsequious courtiers complain that I work in squalor and in secrecy. All I have to apologize for is the smell.

It's said you have no decent pupils to whom you might delegate work because you don't brook any rivals.

I'm proud of the fact that I've never kept a shop, churning out altarpieces and the usual knick-knacks. It's hardly my fault if I can't get the staff. Everyone goes on about Raphael's productivity, but the bigger his workshop got, the worse his work became. Just look at Raphael's fresco of Cupid and

Psyche. It's a disgrace for a great artist, and mostly painted by his pupil Giulio Romano. Delegation just gave Raphael more time to spend with his mistress, and fornication finished him off at the ripe old age of 37. And just what did the great Giulio go on to do?—the drawings for *I Modi*, the world's first set of pornographic prints. My pupils may not be great artists, but they've never disgraced themselves.

You, on the other hand, have raised the status of the artist. Are you not far richer than any previous artist, on a par with the minor nobility?

It's true that I have from time to time been rewarded for my considerable pains, but I'd always expect good work to be so rewarded. I more than earned every ducat that I was paid by Pope Julius and his heirs for the tomb. I'm of noble stock, descended from the

Counts of Canossa, and my fame and fortune have merely enabled me to restore my family to its rightful status and glory. I never sought money or fame for myself. As long as an artist strives to be rich (which today's artists all do), he'll always remain a poor creature. I'd be mortified if I'd raised the status of artists in general—my work should just sound the death-knell for bad artists.

DESPOTS AND DEMOCRATS

During the 19th century, when Italians were striving to create a unified, self-governing nation for the first time, they looked back at Michelangelo as a national hero because of his republican sympathies, and his statue of *David* became a symbol of political freedom. The truth is more complicated, not least because the vast majority of his work was made for despots (like the Medici) and for despotic popes. More recently, the tendency has been to deride Michelangelo for his political maneuverings, a criticism that seems sanctimonious and anachronistic. The wonder is that Michelangelo stood his political ground as firmly as he did.

Maestro, it's been said to me that you're a political opportunist whose political affiliation depends on which way the wind blows.

Oh, you've been listening to the armchair moralists! Those who have never feared for their lives are very good at lecturing those who have. They are the real cowards, because they lack humility and compassion. In an ideal world, I'd be a republican, like any true citizen of Florence. The *commune*—the city state ruled by an elected body of citizens—is the bedrock of Florentine, and of Italian, greatness. Now Italy is enslaved by tyrants, and only Venice retains its freedom (though her artists are still rubbish). When I say I'm a republican, I don't mean I believe in mob rule by those who haven't attained citizenship. We all have our allotted positions in the great chain of being, and the common people are incapable of rational judgment, least of all in politics. Women should, of course, concern themselves with domestic issues, unless they're of exceptional nobility and piety. I believe in oligarchic republics, with joint rule by those qualified to rule. This means a broad coalition of the leading families, as you have in Venice—the city I went to after leaving Piero de' Medici.

How do you justify working for the Medici if you have republican sympathies?

What do you mean by "justify"? Art is its own justification and should contribute to the moral education of man. The ancients believed that statues and paintings of virtuous men and their deeds would inspire those who saw them. If you make good work for a bad man he becomes a little better. The real trouble with our age is that there isn't enough good art. As for the Medici, it's hard to generalize. Rule by a tyrant can sometimes be as enlightened as republican rule, and my first lord, Lorenzo de' Medici, brought peace and prosperity to Florence and Italy for many years. However, even the best tyrants are often succeeded by less able sons, and Piero brought disaster upon us all. Since republican rule is more broadly based, republics are more likely to be stable in the long run, as is proved by Venice. I fled there in my youth because the French army was in Tuscany and looked set to sack Florence. In the event Girolamo Savonarola saved the day and persuaded the French not to attack, but if they had, I wouldn't have made much difference, even armed with my hammer and chisel!

When you created the Medici Chapel, instead of making effigies of Lorenzo and his brother Giuliano, you chose to

make grandiose statues of their extremely insignificant
descendants, also named Lorenzo and Giuliano. Both
died young, achieving little, and both were central
figures in the Medici regime that besieged Florence and
overthrew the first Republic. Yet you glorified them. Why?

This whole discussion is absurd. How do you know
which Lorenzo and which Giuliano they are? They
aren't portraits (which I despise), and what would
be the point of doing accurate likenesses when in
a thousand years no one will know what they looked
like anyway? I chose to give them a grandeur,
proportion, and dignity that would win them greater
praise—and, above all, that would inspire future
generations to be virtuous. Giuliano holds coins
in his hand and is about to dispense charity, while
Lorenzo has a closed money-box to show he's
working out who's most deserving of charity. They're

looking across at a statue of the Virgin and Child, asking for forgiveness and guidance. Any Christian should approve of this.

The Medici Chapel was commissioned by the first Medici pope, Leo X, and most of my career since 1505 has been spent working for the popes. But when I work for the pope, who's almost always a member of a leading Italian family, I work for the office founded by St. Peter, not the mortal who holds that office temporarily. God is my inspiration and my judge, not any individual patron. The Sistine Chapel and St. Peter's are gifts to God, to do with as He pleases—and I have every confidence He won't let them repaint the *Last Judgment*.

But what would God think of your statue of Apollo, *made for Baccio Valori, the terrorizer of Florence and destroyer of her liberties? It's perhaps your most beguiling work.*

I knew this would come up. The Medici were thrown out of Florence in 1527, and I opted to stay and support a new Republic. I immediately stopped work on the Medici Chapel, and when the city was besieged by pro-Medici troops I was put in charge of its fortifications. It's true I fled briefly to Venice when I thought traitors in Florence were going to betray the city, and for this I was declared a rebel, but anyone will tell you I did a very good job on my return. Florence was eventually betrayed in 1530, and I went into hiding, fearing for my life. Baccio Valori was appointed governor of the city, and conducted cruel reprisals. He issued an order for my assassination. I was saved in the nick of time when the second Medici pope, Clement VII, pardoned me.

If you look closely at my *Apollo* you'll see that he's drawing the arrow from his quiver with his left hand, which makes him a left-handed archer.

This is a reference to the so-called Delian Apollo, a benign image of a god famed for his ruthlessness that's found on antique coins. By using his weaker left hand to draw the bowstring, Apollo shows that he's slow to punish and to do harm. What could be more instructive for a vicious brute like Baccio? You mustn't forget, too, that I also made a bust of the tyrant-slayer Brutus to celebrate the murder of Baccio's boss, Duke Alessandro de' Medici, who wanted me dead.

So you think the critics have got you wrong?

Because I'm famous, wealthy, devout, passionate, and opinionated, and because I aim high, people are only too ready to snipe. They just want artists to be seen and not heard—docile production-liners like Raphael and Titian. Let me tell you something—

whenever there's an outbreak of plague, the rich head for their villas in the hills. No one rattles on about this, though I can tell you that country folk are none too pleased, as they often bring the plague with them. I never brought death to anyone by running away.

DEPICTIONS OF WOMEN

In 1557, the Venetian writer Lodovico Dolce said that while Michelangelo was supreme in the depiction of muscular male nudes in violent motion, he was incapable of depicting any other kind of figure, and especially not women (a subject which was, of course, a Venetian speciality). Ever since, people have sought to explain, with varying degrees of sympathy, why his women aren't more feminine or maternal, with psychoanalysts pointing unconvincingly to the early death of his mother. One thing at least is clear: Michelangelo's women are not the product of an imaginative failure. Rather, they are central to the drama of his work.

Maestro, one of the most striking things about your work is the way in which you depict women …

Oh, not that subject again! I know exactly what you're going to say. That my women look like men, that I don't know what a woman's body really looks like, that my Virgin Marys aren't maternal, that the breasts of *Night* in the Medici Chapel look like stuck-on melons …

Let's start with the Virgin Mary.

When I was young, Florentine artists depicted the Virgin in fashionable garments and jewelry, heavily made-up and smiling flirtatiously, playing silly games with the Christ child. It was only with the arrival of the great Dominican Savonarola in our midst that anyone seemed to see anything scandalous in this. The friar fulminated against these air-headed impostors. He said the Virgin Mary was dressed simply and modestly like a poor girl, and not like a whore. I try to give the Virgin the requisite dignity and decorum.

Yes, but your Virgins are not just dressed simply, they're physically very big and imposing

The Virgin Mary is responsible for bearing and rearing the son of God. She'll become a symbol of the Church, and is often described by theologians as the one true column of God's temple. She's hardly going to be a waif. She's a pillar, a cathedral, and a mountain. She has to be of heroic scale.

But this makes her not just rather remote from us, the viewer of the artwork, she's also rather remote from the Christ child. Why isn't she more maternal?

She's not like a real mother—though having said
that, "real" mothers can be pretty remote themselves
when they pack us off to wet-nurses, or die young,
like my own mother, whom I barely knew. The Virgin
knows the divine plan in advance, and it's her duty to
enable Christ to fulfill his mission on earth. Knowing
he's going to be crucified, she has to exercise restraint
and keep her emotions in check. She can't delay or
divert him. Savonarola insisted—correctly in my
view—that the Virgin conducted herself with great
dignity during Christ's Passion, and didn't swoon
or cry. My own Virgins conduct themselves with a
similar restraint during Christ's childhood. They
tend and support but don't cuddle or cocoon him.

Poor old Leonardo knew all this, but being a
sentimentalist at heart he did an elaborate fudge. He

often included St. Anne, the mother of the Virgin, in his Virgin and Child images, and got them to do a sort of "good demon, bad demon" routine. So a smiling Virgin plays with her son, while a stern St. Anne sits behind her and tries to restrain her, sometimes jabbing her finger in the air to remind her of the divine plan. My own Virgins are like a composite of Leonardo's Virgin and St. Anne—ineffable beauty is combined with unerring intelligence and unflinching devotion to duty. They're far more moving, because *we* know that *they* know exactly what's at stake.

Physically, though, some of your women do look rather masculine, especially your female nudes. Is this because you use male models?

Most of the time it's true that we use young boys as models for women, but I've used female models as well. Some of my women have been objects of desire. My Eve from the temptation scene on the Sistine Ceiling, and *Dawn* in the Medici Chapel, have been much admired by sensualists. I've been told that Titian used the pose of Eve in reverse in a fresco in Padua, while *Dawn* is now almost universally treated as a kind of pin-up. The Venetian writer Anton Francesco Doni got very excited about *Night*. Still, I really don't approve of lasciviousness.

Let me explain. I've always loathed the Pygmalion myth. Indeed, it's the single aspect of ancient art and aesthetics that I find least satisfactory. In case you don't know, the sculptor Pygmalion couldn't find the girl of his dreams, so he made a statue of his ideal woman, dressed and undressed her, took her to bed, and so on. Eventually, Venus turned the statue into a real woman, and they lived happily ever after. The Pygmalion myth reduces art to the status of sex-toy, and we do actually hear lots of stories of the ancients pleasuring themselves with statues of Venus. The Venetians revisit the Pygmalion myth with their insipid reclining female nudes. For me, desire has to be mixed with awe and even a little fear if it's to be more than bestial—and more than transitory. Some of Dante's greatest and most impassioned poems were addressed to a so-called *"donna petrosa"*—a stony woman who's as formidable as she is beautiful, and whose obduracy inflames Dante's passion further. My women aren't men in drag—they just have an irreducible stony core that inspires adoration. Even when naked, they don't allow a presumption of intimacy.

Some of your men have a delicacy and grace about them that's almost feminine. It's as though typically feminine qualities have migrated to your men.

The ancients believed that men and women were originally joined together, but when they misbehaved, God separated them, and so our life is spent in search of our other half. Remember, too, that Eve was made from one of Adam's ribs, so Eve was, if you like, latent in Adam. For a man to retain a hint of feminine delicacy is to be still in a state of grace—so long as he doesn't lapse into effeminacy. A bit of virility does the same for women. It universalizes them.

My first statue of a god, the *Bacchus*, was hermaphroditic, and this underpinned the wine-god's irresistible power and appeal. But perhaps the most grandly feminine of my figures is the statue of Giuliano de' Medici in the Medici Chapel. He has long, languid fingers, a dainty head on a long neck, and big strong breasts. Giuliano's great breasts show that he's an ideal ruler who serves as both

mother and father to his people. He exemplifies
St. Bernard's belief that those in command should,
as it were, expose their breasts and let their bosoms
expand with milk, not swell with passion. Now look
at this drawing (*holding one up*). Next to some studies
for the grotesque decoration on Giuliano's armor,
I've drawn a caricature of a young woman suckling
on an old man's breast ...

GIANT SIZE AND SCALE

Michelangelo is associated with figures of superhuman scale and size, and with projects that grew ever more ambitious as he worked on them. Usually, he found receptive ears and purses, none more so than the irascible Pope Julius II, who needed no encouragement to emulate the ancient Romans. The ambitions of Julius' Medici successors, Leo X and Clement VII, centered on the Medici family church of San Lorenzo. But even Michelangelo balked at Clement's proposal to build a colossus around 80 feet high by the church, drily suggesting the statue might incorporate a barber's shop, dovecote, and bell tower.

Maestro, if you compare your work with that of your 15th-century predecessors and with that of your contemporaries, one's immediately struck by the fact that it's much bigger. This is particularly obvious with your statues.

It's not just a question of size—it's a question of scale. Even when I carve a Christ child that's only a couple of feet tall, he seems more imposing than a figure of equivalent size by, say, Verrocchio, Botticelli, or Raphael, because of his grander proportions.

He looks like a baby Hercules.

Yes, exactly. I do prefer my figures to be over life-size—except, of course, in drawings. This relates to my hatred of the Pygmalion myth. I want viewers to feel awe as well as desire. When I was a boy, there was a craze for making bronze statuettes and medals with antique subject matter. Bertoldo, who was in charge of the Medici sculpture garden, was a specialist in small bronzes, and they very much appealed to Lorenzo de' Medici, who had a big collection of antique statuettes, plaquettes, medals, and cameos. I wasn't interested in making the sort of trinket that could fit on a table or shelf, or could be put in a drawer—when all's said and done, Bertoldo's statuette of Apollo playing a *lira da braccio* is not much better than a dildo.

The ancients most valued statues of colossal scale. You must have heard of the Colossus of Rhodes, a standing figure, 105 feet tall, through whose parted legs ships could sail. When I was in Carrara quarrying marble for the Julius tomb in 1505, I was tempted to carve out of a mountain overlooking the sea a colossus that would have been visible from afar to seafarers. This was the madness of youth, and in four lifetimes I would never have been able to complete it! But the principle is sound—always aspire to epic rather than domestic scale.

Your largest statue is the David. *It's nearly 14 feet high and stands on a large base. But it's not only bigger than, say, Donatello's* David, *which is about 5 feet tall. Your* David *is also quite a bit older. He is post- rather than pre-pubescent.*

Theologians say that David marks the beginning of a new epoch, the start of the manhood of God's chosen people. His faith in God allows him to grow, and gives him a stature that's more than a match for any giant. Christ is traditionally known as the "Son of David," because Joseph is David's descendant, so I also wanted to show the perfect body and genitals from which Christ ultimately issued. You couldn't do this with a little urchin.

But in the Bible, and in theology, small is often more beautiful than big. The whole point of the David and Goliath story is that he's a pint-sized shepherd boy, armed only with a sling. This is exactly how you depict him in a corner of the Sistine Ceiling. And the same virile manhood that ultimately engendered Christ also committed adultery with Bathsheba, and arranged for her husband to be assassinated.

You're wondering which David I've given you—the boy wonder who kills Goliath, the ancestor of Christ, or the sexual predator. I'm giving you the whole package. In my work colossal size and scale don't just make the actions seem more heroic, they intensify the drama. I do want you to wonder if my giants are about to overreach themselves, or whether they have an Achilles heel.

Christian writers have certainly given giants a bad press. Dante has five giants chained up in the pit of Hell, including Nimrod, builder of the Tower of Babel. A Florentine mathematician estimated that Nimrod must have been about 82 feet tall, using the hints offered by Dante. When I was painting the *Last Judgment* I wrote a poem about a Nimrod-style giant who sets up high towers to reach heaven, but he can't see heaven because he has only one eye set in his heel. In another poem two giants are so tall they've blinded themselves by gazing into the sun. The *Last Judgment* is 45 feet high, so I was sometimes anxious that I, too, was overreaching myself. Biagio da Cesena had already started a whispering campaign against the fresco. And I did in fact injure myself falling off the scaffolding.

In your statues, isn't the fear that your giants might have overreached themselves, and may be heading for a fall, combined with the fear they might literally fall over?

I carve my statues in such a way that it appears near-miraculous that they're still standing, especially because of their often vigorous movement and enlarged torsos, which give them a high center of gravity. We're more wary of getting close to a large statue than to a large painting, simply because of the fear that it might fall on us. Statues that inexplicably fall down are a staple of folk tales, and are taken as omens of terrible events. You sometimes hear stories of sacred pictures starting to bleed, but this is usually only if they've been deliberately vandalized. As a result, people are more wary of getting close to a large statue than to a large painting. The first statue I made in Rome addressed the issue of stability head on. It was an over-life-size statue of the wine-god Bacchus, and he's very drunk indeed. People usually give it a wide berth because he's lolling around. I recently wrote a poem about a figure trapped inside a great boulder that falls off a mountainside, and ends up in a lowly place among a heap of stones. All my statues are literally and metaphorically imbued with this fear of ending up in a heap of stones. The bigger they are, the more vulnerable they are, and the further they have to fall.

So the achievement of colossal size and scale is a dangerous high-wire act? And one that can't be performed by statuettes?

If a statuette topples from a desk, which they regularly do, it's like a toddler falling over—no bones are broken, no empires fall.

MARBLE MANIA

Leonardo da Vinci spoke for many of his
contemporaries when he derided the art of
sculpture, describing it as a largely mechanical
exercise in which sculptors got all sweaty and
emerged from their workshops covered in
white marble dust so that they looked like
bakers. Conversely, he claimed that painting
was a gentlemanly art that could be practiced in
comfort at home. Michelangelo challenged this
prejudice against back-breaking physical labor,
not only by taking sculpture to unimaginable
heights, but also by wearing his sculptor's
badge with pride. In his poems he turned stone-
carving into a quasi-mystical rite.

Maestro, didn't Leonardo dismiss sculpture …

(*Interrupting the question*) How boring can you get?
Leonardo kept saying this when he was a sort of
court jester in Milan, and conspicuously failing to
complete an equestrian statue. But he's typical of
his age. All his big public and quasi-public projects
were screw-ups, and it was only really his drawings
that amounted to anything. Needing an alibi for his
failures on a large scale, he contrived to argue that
any art form that required serious muscular exertion
or application must be inferior, and could certainly
not be pursued by a gentleman. Easel painting was
best because it could be done in a fine house, wearing
elegant clothes, and while listening to music. It's
nothing less than a manifesto for the domesticated
bourgeois art that dominated taste in the second half
of the 15th century. But when you hit rock bottom,

the only way is up, and I answered the need for an art that had balls, and which reached for the stars. My *David* is a case in point. The huge marble block was originally given to Agostino di Duccio in the 1460s, but as he specialized in small reliefs populated by charming tailor's dummies, he botched it, and it wasn't until I came on the scene that anyone could handle it. It was like a new dawn—here at last was some art with presence that you could really look up to.

You also set great store by getting the marble at source— no great artist has spent so much time in the quarries.

I first came to love quarries from my visits to Settignano. It brought home to me the importance of finding suitable and flawless blocks of marble. It's dangerous and time-consuming work. Carrara is a good day's ride from Florence, and then there's a long climb to the quarry. A man was killed, and I just missed being killed, when an iron ring snapped and a large block slid down a slope, smashing to smithereens. Transporting the block from the quarry by cart and boat is equally hazardous. In some respects quarrying is a parallel enterprise to anatomical dissection—it's traditionally been regarded as piercing the entrails of the earth, seeking out good veins of marble. For me, the whole experience is a cross between a pilgrimage and the Labors of Hercules.

You insist on working from a single block.

The ancients did too, and Pliny gives particular praise for large sculptures made from a single block. There's a good practical reason for this. As soon as

you put separate pieces of stone together, there's
a greater chance of rain and moisture getting into
the joins. But there are even better spiritual and
conceptual reasons. A statue made from paring
down a single block has more integrity and intensity.
Lorenzo de' Medici wrote poetry and he said the
sonnet was the equal of all other poetic forms because
of the greater difficulty of saying what you have to
say in the space of fourteen lines. My *David* is nearly
14 feet high, but I like to think he has the compact
intensity of a great poem. This creation involved huge
amounts of brainwork and not just brawn, for with
marble you can't correct mistakes. With sculpture
in bronze, and with painting, there's a far greater
risk that the artwork will be diffuse, because you can
revise and add on piecemeal ad infinitum. That's
what tended to happen in the 15th century. Then
you got those ridiculous proposals by Leon Battista

Alberti and by Leonardo for machines that would enable you to make multi-part sculptures. When the damaged marble block for the *David* was resuscitated, my proposal was the only one not to involve adding new pieces. In the past, they even used to paint marble sculpture, further polluting it.

One of the surprising things about your many poems which refer to the visual arts is that quite a few refer to sculpture made of metal. You're not totally fixated on making stone sculpture, then?

I've made several bronze sculptures—above all, my seated effigy of Pope Julius in Bologna, and a bronze statue of David that was sent to France. I've also made a few designs for goldsmiths, including a salt-cellar for the duke of Urbino. But I do think marble sculpture is fundamentally superior. In my poems, what interests me is the heat used in the process of making metal sculpture. Goldsmiths and bronze casters need fire because the metal has to be molten before it can flow into the mold or be hammered. Carving stone is a "cold" procedure, apart from the sparks that occasionally fly off the chisel. Fire is fatal to marble and turns it into lime. But I like to think I've infused my marble statues with a life-giving fire and warmth, and that I've sometimes made marble appear to melt and flow.

Earlier you let me see a woodcut illustration in a book of popular astrology that showed you as an exemplary "saturnine" sculptor. You're a wild man, clad only in a loin-cloth, about to impale your chisel in the breast of the Medici Chapel Dawn. *When you tackle a large marble block, is it a sublimated form of single combat?*

We live in an increasingly anonymous and impersonal age. Battles are now fought from a distance by indistinguishable foot soldiers. Books appear in vast print runs of identical copies. Art is multiplied and mass-produced in engravings and casts. My sculpture is the record of an unrepeatable encounter between one God-fearing man and nature.

PAINTING HIMSELF

Michelangelo claimed not to be a painter, but
there is little sign of this in the Sistine Chapel.
The Sistine Ceiling is the first great ceiling
painting: before this, the only ceiling scenes
with large figures were medieval mosaics, like
San Marco in Venice. The fashion at the time
was for decorative coffered ceilings, with small
narrative pictures squeezed in the gaps, and this
was what Pope Julius initially asked for. It was
Michelangelo who proposed doing something
unprecedented. The Sistine Ceiling, and the
Last Judgment, were hugely influential, with
Michelangelo's figure types parachuted into
the work of other artists almost before his
paint was dry.

We're standing in the Sistine Chapel and we're looking up at the two greatest frescoes of all time—both painted by Michelangelo Buonarroti.

Not so loud. This is a place of worship.

(Whispering) Sorry, Maestro ... Despite these amazing achievements, you always insist that painting is not your profession.

It's certainly true that I learned the basics about painting in the Ghirlandaio workshop, and assisted on some of their frescoes and altarpieces. But once I'd gone to the Medici sculpture garden I always thought of myself as a sculptor. I signed my letters "Michelangelo, sculptor." My conviction that sculpture was my profession intensified when I was diverted from Pope Julius' tomb to paint the Sistine Ceiling. In truth, I was also trying to protect myself in case I failed, which many influential people thought I would—Bramante, the architect of the new St. Peter's, said I wouldn't be able to paint foreshortened figures. Foreshortened figures were the least of my worries. I'd never painted a fresco on my own before, and no one else had painted a ceiling fresco of such scale and ambition. My fresco replaced a decorative painted canopy of stars on a blue background, painted by an anonymous artisan. You can understand why they kept things simple: the vault measures around 45×128 feet, has various kinds of curved surface, is not entirely regular, and rises over 60 feet above the ground. I stood on a gantry to paint aided by lamplight, arching my back, sticking my butt out, getting spattered by drips of paint. Most of the work— except for preparing the surfaces, grinding pigment, and painting the trompe-l'oeil architecture—was done by me alone. I badly strained my eyes and my neck. The physical and mental exertion nearly finished me off, and I wasn't helped by Pope Julius, who delayed the completion of the second half by withholding funds.

So you're not against painting per se?

I'm against Flemish painting, which is completely overrunning us. The two great diseases of our time are the French pox and Flemish painting. Some people say that God was a painter, painting the world into existence, but you can't imagine Him sitting down before an easel in fine clothes, fretting neurotically over minute details, repainting ad nauseam. It took Him seven days to create the entire universe. How many years did Leonardo spend painting the upper third of that smug Florentine housewife? I spent a single day painting the scene of God separating light from darkness.

The art of fresco, perfected by Giotto and Masaccio, *is* Italian painting. Fresco is the great gift from God that was given to no other country. It favors the strong and the single-minded. You can only work while the plaster's wet. If you make a mistake, you have to scrape off the plaster and start again. You have to be a great draftsman and a bold colorist. You need perseverance to see it, too—look up for long at this ceiling and you'll get eye-strain and a crooked neck. No wonder fresco's a dying art.

We talked before about Adam and the male nudes. Can you say something about the seven Hebrew Prophets and the five pagan Sybils—the biggest and most eye-catching figures on the entire ceiling?

They're crucial figures, because they prophesied
the coming of Christ. They prove that God and his
divine plan are discernible to any man or woman,
at any time or place. Some are a bit fidgety because
they're excited by their visions, others because
they can't quite believe their inner eyes. Like most
of the figures on the vault, they become progressively
larger as they approach the altar. Those at the
entrance are just under 13 feet high, those over
the altar just over 14½ feet. I've given them an
almost planetary rotundity and amplitude to suggest
the way in which prophecies stretch across time
and space.

The most important—and unencumbered—of the
figures is Jonah, positioned directly over the altar.
Jonah is psychologically the most complex of the
prophets. When God told him to go and chastise the
pagan citizens of Nineveh for their wickedness, he

ran away and was swallowed by a giant fish. Inside its belly he prayed for forgiveness, and so God made the fish vomit him up after three days and nights. This was prophetic of Christ's resurrection. Jonah was then furious with God for forgiving the Ninevites after they decided to repent. My Jonah wears only a loin cloth and a sleeveless vest, and he twists back and sideways to stare up accusingly at God, convulsed in anger. In terms of foreshortening, this is the most ambitious figure I've ever made, because the curve of Jonah's body contradicts the curve of the ceiling. But it's not just art for art's sake—contradiction, and defiance of logic, is what Jonah is about.

Do you identify with him?

We have a saying that "every painter paints himself," meaning that an artist's physical and mental idiosyncrasies will be projected onto the work they are doing—unless they take great care to suppress them. So when someone once asked me why a painter was better at painting cattle than anything else, I replied that every painter paints himself well. I certainly do think Jonah is a fascinating personality, and painting the Sistine Ceiling did feel a bit like being stuck in the belly of a big fish. But the main point about this particular episode is that it's the only occasion in the Old Testament when God forgave a pagan civilization. It tells us that it's never too late to reform our ways and to join the true Church.

What about the Last Judgment?

The *Last Judgment* says what Last Judgments always say. On the last day, we'll be resurrected, our bones clothed in flesh, and then we'll be damned or saved.

With its uninflected deep blue background, it has a heraldic clarity to it, don't you think? Blue pigment comes from lapis lazuli, and costs a small fortune—but it's worth every ducat.

TO FINISH OR NOT TO FINISH

Around two-thirds of Michelangelo's surviving sculptures and panel paintings are unfinished—a uniquely high proportion. Michelangelo's contemporaries were both fascinated and exasperated by this phenomenon. In modern times, there has been a tendency to prefer the unfinished to the finished sculptures, the assumption being that they offer an intimate glimpse of the creative process. This is wonderfully illustrated by Michelangelo's unfinished *St. Matthew*, which shows how he worked from the front of the marble block to the back. His own views on the matter are contradictory, but his uncertainty is symptomatic of an age that was beginning to collect drawings and sketch-models.

The sheer quantity of your unfinished work is quite amazing. I wonder if you can explain why this has happened?

If it wasn't for the tragedy of Pope Julius' tomb, I'd never have a reputation for not finishing. I've only ever wanted to be allowed to complete the tomb. The first proposal would have been one of the wonders of the world. But Bramante, who wanted Pope Julius' last ducat to be spent on the new St. Peter's, scuppered the project, and since then various popes have monopolized my time, ensuring that in each revised contract the tomb shrunk in size.

The final version in San Pietro in Vincoli is dominated by the statue of Moses, which I finished painstakingly. There would have been many more statues like it, were it not for the impossible pressures. Given these, I think it's extraordinary

how much work I *have* completed, with few
discernible dips in quality.

You've undoubtedly been a victim of your own success,
and this explains why some of your commissions were
never fulfilled. But you gave away two unfinished
statues from the first scheme for Pope Julius' tomb,
the Dying Slave *and the* Awakening Slave, *to Roberto*
Strozzi, in gratitude for taking you into his home
during two serious illnesses. This doesn't suggest
embarrassment or shame at unfinished work.

Everyone seems to have their own view about all this.
Vasari said I'm such a perfectionist that I'm rarely
satisfied with my work, but this usually only happens
if the marble has a flaw, or if there's an unavoidable
change in plan, as regularly occurred with the tomb.
Condivi said the rough surfaces of the unfinished

statues in the Medici Chapel don't interfere with the beauty of the work, implying that I'd taken them as far as they needed to go. I'm not entirely sure what I think, and I have to be very careful in case anyone assumes I'm advocating dilatoriness.

Donatello was the first artist to exploit rough surface effects, especially in his late work. I told Condivi that Donatello's only fault was that he lacked patience in polishing his works, so that while a statue like *Judith and Holofernes* looks great from a distance, it's less successful when seen close up. But I now disagree. I should have told Condivi that when works are good, they don't need much polishing. That said, it's undoubtedly easier for sophisticated connoisseurs like Roberto Strozzi to interpret the less finished parts than it is for the masses. I wouldn't want the *Slaves* put in the Piazza della Signoria with the *David*.

Over the fireplace, I can see one of your first sculptures,
the unfinished relief, Battle of the Centaurs. *I know*
you're very proud of it. Why have you kept it all this time,
and why isn't it finished?

It was made for Lorenzo de' Medici, and I stopped
working on it when he died. I still think it's perfect,
and every time I see it I realize what a natural and
instinctive sculptor I am. I could have finished it
off quite easily, polishing it up a bit, and giving
more definition to the hair. But I do like the visual
rhyme between the round rocks which some of the
combatants are holding, and their roughly carved
heads. The seated man in the bottom lefthand corner
of the sculpture holds his head, but he could almost
be holding a rock. This ambiguity intensifies the
feeling that we're watching a murderous bunch of
blockheads.

*You do seem rather intrigued by the relationship—
sometimes empowering, sometimes debilitating—
between raw rock and the nude male body. Your
landscape settings are invariably rocky, as though
your protagonists lived in a Stone Age. And in your
poems, you're clearly fascinated by the rough, stony
husk that "contains" the statue.*

Every sculptor has to be fully aware of the entire
marble block. I tend to draw the outline of the
figures on the front face, and then gradually work
from front to back. That way, you can at least make
some adjustments as you go. In my unfinished
statue of *St. Matthew*, the projecting knee is the
most finished part.

*But in your poems, you often express the relationship
between man and his environment in terms of a*

relationship between flesh and stone. The stony
husk is far more than just packaging, to be cut away
and disposed of.

I suppose you must be thinking of the poem we discussed earlier in which the speaker is a "figure" enclosed within a great boulder on a mountain side. The stone block initially seems to be a kind of protective covering, like a hermit's cave. But then, against the man's will, the boulder rolls all the way down the mountainside, ending up in a "low place" in a "pile of stones." Suddenly, he's thrust into the world, and the world presses in hard on all sides. Perhaps the rough stone surrounding *St. Matthew* is both protective and predatory. It's certainly nothing like Leonardo's *sfumato*, which is an indiscriminate blurring effect that makes everything soft and soupy.

There's an energizing friction between finished and unfinished parts. With the Slaves, there's an almost sadomasochistic relish about the juxtaposition of smooth flesh and rough stone. In the late Crucifixion drawings, the incessantly redrawn contours clothe the figures like a visual hair shirt …

Hold your horses! This interview is careening out of control. I take back everything I've said. Let's start from the top, and let me spell it out for you: nothing pains me more than to see unfinished statues.

HEAVEN OR HELL

When Michelangelo died, he was treated like a
saint, with Florentines filing past to touch his
corpse. Our main written source for his spiritual
life is his poems, though most of the specifically
religious ones date from the later part of his
life, when he was friendly with Vittoria Colonna,
and was working on the *Last Judgment* and the
rebuilding of St. Peter's. He seems to have been
sympathetic to church reform as first advocated
by Savonarola, but it is unclear what he felt
about the Reformation. His late depictions of
the dead Christ are now regarded as the most
spiritually intense works of art ever made.

Maestro, religion has cropped up repeatedly in our talks,
in a way that I can't imagine happening with Raphael
or Titian, and especially with Leonardo.

Even when the subject matter is religious, most
of today's art is materialist and secular. I believe
I may be the last religious artist. As a young man,
I was greatly moved by Savonarola. I went to hear
his sermons in Florence Cathedral, and read them
when they were published. I can still hear his voice,
holding imaginary dialogues with the Devil, or
suddenly addressing a section of the audience—
"Hey you, tepid one!" "Hey you, money bags!"
"Hey you, sodomite!" The last sermon I heard
before fleeing Florence for the first time made
my hair stand on end, and climaxed with the
piercing cry: "I shall spill flood waters over the
earth." When I was painting the Sistine Ceiling,

and Pope Julius was away fighting in central Italy,
I wrote a poem inspired by Savonarola, lamenting
that in present-day Rome, helmets and swords are
made from chalices, and Christ's blood is sold by
the bucketful.

You returned only briefly to Florence when Savonarola
was the spiritual leader of the Republic. There you made
a sculpture of a sleeping Cupid, which you palmed off
as an antiquity, before heading for Rome to carve a
Bacchus. Isn't there a contradiction here? These works
don't seem very Christian.

A sleeping Cupid signifies the passing of earthly
pleasures, and you forget I also carved a statue of
St. John the Baptist. The Florentine economy was
in turmoil, and Savonarola made the climate even
more unfavorable for patronage by his attacks on

indulgence and immorality, which resulted in the so-called "bonfires of vanities." I'm sure if he'd understood what I was doing a little better, things might have been different. But he was certainly quite right to burn all that modern rubbish. I went to Rome because I was summoned by a cardinal of the Church, Raffaelle Riario. There was nothing irreligious or indecent about the *Bacchus*. His drunkenness prefigures the delirium experienced by Christ during his Passion, and wine is a Eucharistic symbol for the redemptive blood of Jesus. This is why I depict the drunkenness of Noah on the Sistine Chapel ceiling. When Savonarola was hanged and burned I was carving my great *Pietà* for the tomb of a French Cardinal.

So you're in sympathy with some of Savonarola's ideas. Are you also in sympathy with the Reformation?

The splitting of the Church into two denominations
is the great tragedy of our time. It could have
been avoided if the Church of Rome had listened
to Savonarola and rooted out corruption and
ignorance. I'm sure he would have approved of my
Last Judgment. It takes up the entire altar wall of the
Sistine Chapel, where conclaves to select new popes
are held, and it reminds the leaders of the Church
what awaits them if they err.

My noble friend Vittoria Colonna was very
sympathetic to some of the aims of the Protestant
reformers, and hoped there'd be a reconciliation.
Like them, she believed that grace couldn't be
received by the worshiper from a priest through the
material sacraments of the Mass—grace depended
solely on man's faith in the justice of Christ.
However, she didn't believe that justification by faith
alone obviated the need for good works, and I, too,

go on pilgrimages and make charitable gifts to the deserving poor. Most of my recent works, including the drawings I did for her, demonstrate my faith in Christ. I've repeatedly depicted Him during and after the Passion—as you can see in this black chalk drawing (*handing it to the interviewer*).

You show Christ on a Y-shaped cross, with two flanking figures walking up from behind. Each contour is redrawn incessantly, as though we are seeing a mirage. Everything trembles and wobbles, even the cross and Christ's head.

I wanted to show people in the process of finding their faith. The idea that God would allow his son to be incarnated and crucified in order to save humanity almost beggars belief. But this blinding truth is about to be fully revealed to the bystanders coming up from behind the cross. As yet everything seems hazy. The man on Christ's left seems especially unsure of where he is and where he's going. I wrote a madrigal for Vittoria Colonna which more or less expresses his predicament. It went something like this: "Now on my right foot, now on my left, shuffling from one to the other, I search for my salvation. My troubled heart moves between vice and virtue, exhausting me. I am like someone who cannot see the sky because along every path it is hidden and lost from view."

How would this reassure people, though? You show us a blurred image of the crucified Christ that may or may not be coming into clearer view. You seem compelled to draw him again and again, and each time he's as blurred as the last. We're a long way from the pin-sharp, athletic body of Christ in the St. Peter's Pietà.

I wanted to express the turmoil that any Christian must feel when they think about the death of Christ. My drawing hand is not as steady as it was, owing to old age, and I'm now long-sighted, but I've exaggerated any unsteadiness for expressive ends.

Do you still believe that art can show us the way?

There's no doubt that humanity is further away than it's ever been from heaven and from spiritual rebirth. Since the French first invaded Italy, one catastrophe has followed hard on the heels of another, and Italy has become the main theater of war in Europe. Savonarola believed this was punishment for our sins. The French didn't just bring state-of-the-art artillery and firearms with them, they brought something far more lethal—syphilis, which we call the French pox. Now even Rome has been sacked and the Reformation has emasculated the papacy. On my stairwell I've drawn a skeleton carrying a coffin, with the following admonitory inscription: "I say to you who have given your body, soul, and spirit to the world: you will end up in this dark coffin." But I still believe there's hope. The clearest part of my drawing is Christ's right hand, and his index finger points upward, showing us the way. And so will the lantern of St. Peter's, when it's finally built.

REFILL?

PRIMARY SOURCES

E.H. Ramsden (trans. and ed.), *The Letters of Michelangelo* (London: Peter Owen, 1963; Stanford: Stanford University Press, 1963) The letters are mostly about business matters, but they give a good idea of Michelangelo's personality.

A few key letters are published in **Creighton Gilbert**, *Complete Poems and Selected Letters of Michelangelo* (Princeton: Princeton University Press, 1964)

Christopher Ryan (trans. and ed.), *Michelangelo, The Poems* (London: J.M. Dent & Sons, 1996) Parallel Italian text and English translation: the most accessible edition.

EARLY BIOGRAPHIES

Ascanio Condivi, *The Life of Michelangelo*, intro. C. Robertson (London: Pallas Athene, 2006) Michelangelo's marginal comments on Condivi's biography appear in **Ascanio Condivi**,

The Life of Michelanglo, trans. and ed. A.S. Wohl (Pennsylvania: Penn State University Press, 1999)

Francisco de Holanda, *Dialogues with Michelangelo*, intro. D. Hemsoll (London: Pallas Athene, 2006)

Giorgio Vasari, *The Life of Michelangelo*, intro. D. Hemsoll (London: Pallas Athene, 2006)

GENERAL WORKS AND CATALOGUES

J.S. Ackerman, *The Architecture of Michelangelo* (London: Penguin Books, 1970) The standard work on the architecture.

G.C. Argan and B. Contardi, *Michelangelo: Architect* (London: Phaidon Press, 2004) Every project is lavishly illustrated, but the text is frequently opaque.

G. Bull, *Michelangelo* (London: Viking, 1995; New York: St. Martin's Griffin, 1998) A useful if pedestrian biography.

J. Hall, *Michelangelo and the Reinvention of the Human Body* (London: Chatto and Windus, 2005; New York: Farrar, Straus, and Giroux, 2005) General survey that pays close attention to the body language of Michelangelo's figures, and issues such as women, scale, and anatomy.

H. Hibbard, *Michelangelo* (London: Allen Lane, 1975; New York: Harper Collins, 1985) Still the best all-round introductory text.

M. Hirst, *Michelangelo and his Drawings* (London and New Haven: Yale University Press, 1988) The standard introduction to this crucial aspect of his work.

A. Hughes, *Michelangelo* (London: Phaidon, 1997) Very well illustrated general introduction; good on historical context.

The Last Judgment: A Glorious Restoration (New York: Harry N. Abrams, Inc., 1997) Lavishly illustrated with useful essays.

C. de Tolnay, *Michelangelo*, 5 vols. (New York: Princeton University Press, 1943–60) The heavy emphasis on Michelangelo's Neoplatonism now seems overstated, but this remains the foundation-stone of modern Michelangelo studies, and it has an unrivaled array of illustrations.

C. de Tolnay, *Corpus dei Disegni di Michelangelo*, 4 vols. (Novara: Istituto Geografico De Agostini, 1975–80) Color facsimiles of every drawing.

P. De Vecchi (ed.), *The Sistine Chapel: A Glorious Restoration* (New York: Harry N. Abrams, Inc., 1999) Lavishly illustrated with useful essays.

W.E. Wallace, *Michelangelo: Selected Scholarship in English*, 5 vols. (London and New York: Garland Science, 1995) A wide selection of modern essays.

J. Wilde, *Michelangelo: Six Lectures*, (Oxford and New York: Oxford University Press, 1978 and 1979) Lucid, probing survey by one of the leading modern scholars.

INDEX